Brave, Stro~~n~~ Leonie
and the Race of a Lifetime

by Hilary Moore
Illustrated by Catty Flores

*Dedicated to all the girls growing up
brave and strong around the world!*

Diversity ✦
Publishing

Illustrations by Catty Flores © 2015 www.cattyflores.com

Published by:

Diversity Publishing
Diversity Publishing is a trade name of Brave Strong Books Ltd
28A Springfield
WD231GL
Bushey Heath
Herts
United Kingdom
www.bravestronggirls.com

Once upon a time, there was a brave, strong village girl called Leonie, who lived among the snow-clad mountains of Asia. Her mother and father named her Leonie because they wanted her to be as brave as a lioness. Leonie was full of determination and joy. Her two best friends were a boy called Jaran and a golden eagle, Kubilai. Above all else, she loved to race Jaran across the mountains on her brave little pony, with Kubilai on her arm.

Nobody else in the village had a Golden Eagle for a friend. Leonie had found Kubilai in the mountains when he was a young chick. The little bird had fallen from his nest and was starving. Leonie built him a new nest in the crook of a cliff and climbed the mountain every day to bring him food. Now he was a huge and mighty hunter. The sight of the two of them playing in the mountains was awesome to behold.

Jaran was the neighbour's little boy, born in the same month as Leonie. They had grown up side by side, like brother and sister, and loved one another very much. Usually, only boys raced on ponies, but when Jaran had started to learn, Leonie had insisted she learn too. As they always did everything together, her parents had agreed and Leonie became a skilled rider.

The day after Jaran's tenth birthday, Leonie went in search of her friend to go riding in the mountains. But she only found his mother and his younger sister at home. When she asked where Jaran was, his mother looked surprised.

"But don't you know?" she asked. "Jaran is now ten. He must prepare with the other boys for the Great Race."

Leonie remembered the Great Race last year. She and Jaran had watched the riders gather with their families, the ponies scuffing the dirt with their hooves, anxious to get started. And then at the drop of a red silk scarf, they were away – thundering into the distance!

She had waited for hours with Jaran at the finishing line. She remembered their excitement as the ponies finally appeared from the distant valleys, galloping towards them, dust flying into the air, everyone screaming support for the leaders. The two friends had always dreamed of riding in the Great Race together.

"Tell me where he is! I will join him!" Leonie gasped with excitement. She began running for her pony, but Jaran's mother stopped her.

"But you are a girl! You can't compete in the Great Race – it's only for boys. You and Jaran have been friends for many years. But now it is time to grow up."

Leonie looked at Jaran's mother, shocked. "But I am a rider. I can ride as fast as Jaran – as fast as any boy! Of course I must race them – I will beat them all!"

Jaran's younger sister smiled, dreaming of competing herself one day, but Jaran's mother shook her head gently. "The village chief will never allow it" she said. Leonie, defiant, ran home, jumped on her pony and headed into the mountains to find Jaran. Kubilai flew after her, his golden wings flashing in the sun.

When she found the boys, she stood on a rock with Kubilai on her arm, watching and waiting. Finally, as the sun was setting, the other boys set out for home, and Jaran came to join her.

s soon as he arrived, he smiled at Leonie's determined face. "You want to race too, don't you?" he said.

"I *must* race," she answered. "We must race together."

"They will never allow it," Jaran protested.

"Who can stop me?" Leonie answered. "We can train secretly every day at sundown. And on the day of the race, I will wear some of your clothes, and cut my hair so they don't notice me until we are at the finishing line."

Standing on the rock, the sun falling behind the mountain, the friends shook hands and made a pact. They would practice every day – pushing each other to be the best they could – so that they could win the Great Race together.

inally, the day came for the boys in the village to race. The riders would battle through thirty miles of mountains under a blazing sun. It was a huge test of endurance, determination and strength, for the ponies and the riders.

As they had planned, Jaran helped Leonie cut her hair short to look just like his. When they were finished, Leonie looked like a proper little mountain boy. She ran her fingers through her hair. "Now it can't get in my eyes when I'm riding as fast as the wind!" she laughed.

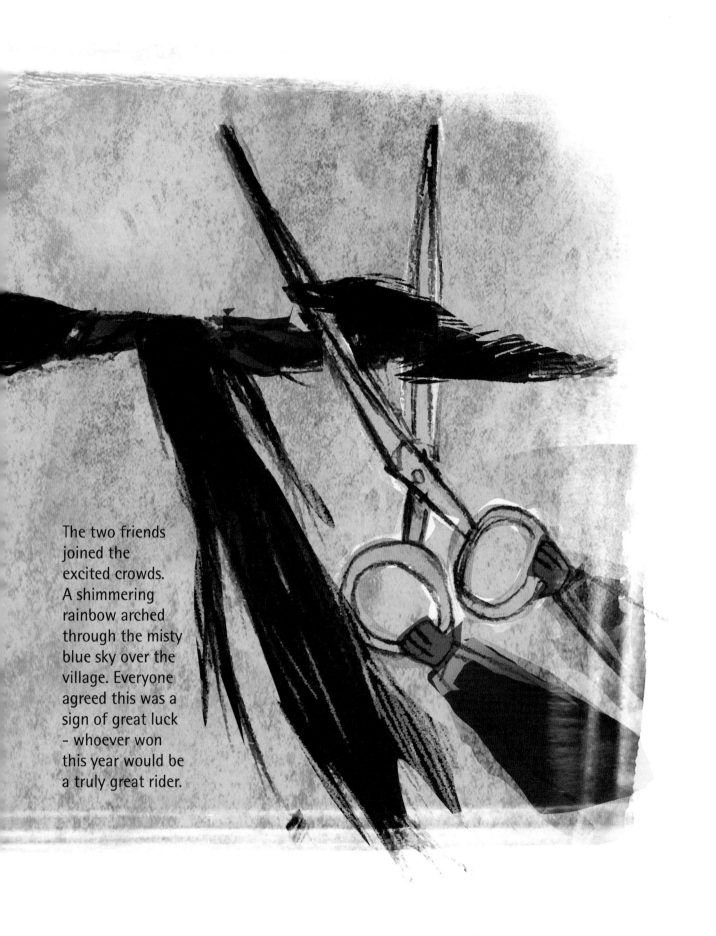

The two friends joined the excited crowds. A shimmering rainbow arched through the misty blue sky over the village. Everyone agreed this was a sign of great luck – whoever won this year would be a truly great rider.

The riders were all clustered around the starting line. There were at least twenty boys from different villages jostling for position, so Leonie was able to push through unnoticed. She could just see the raised arm with the red silk scarf floating in the sky, waiting. Her heart began to race with excitement. And then the words:

"On your marks...... Get Set...... GO!"

The silk scarf fell to the ground and they were off. The crowds cheered and shouted as the riders raced towards the hills, their ponies' hooves thudding against the ground. Kubilai, powerful and serene, watched them from above.

The first hour of the race was the most exciting of their lives. The ponies raced across the plains in a whirlwind of dust and dashed up and down the narrow mountain trails, their tails flying. Gradually the best riders began to pull ahead. Leonie and Jaran were both up front, with five others.

They were coming up to a wide stream. Leonie knew from her practice that she had to start jumping at the perfect time, or her pony would fall in the water. She was riding faster than ever before as she hurtled towards the stream. She urged her pony into the jump and was over in perfect stride – pulling out in front of the others.

She turned to smile at Jaran but couldn't see him. Then she heard Kubilai screeching to her from above. That was the call he used for danger. She looked back and saw Kubilai swooping to the ground and saw Jaran, who had been thrown from his horse, standing at the side of the stream.

Before she knew it, the other horses had passed her. She looked desperately at the riders as they charged into the distance, but she couldn't leave Jaran so far from home. Turning, she galloped back towards the stream.

Jaran waved to her to turn. "I'm fine – my stirrup broke – Go! Go!" he shouted.

But Leonie was determined not to leave him alone on the mountainside. She threw herself off her pony and pulled it to join Jaran's, letting them drink from the stream.

"It will help them go faster" she said. "I'm lighter than you – I can ride without a saddle. We can swap. You're sure you're not hurt?"

Jaran shouted that he was fine and leapt onto Leonie's pony. "You're sure?" he asked.

"Yes!" answered Leonie. She pulled the saddle off Jaran's pony and threw herself up on its back. "Let's go!" she cried. The ponies had drunk just enough to get their energy back, and were flying forward a moment later. The leaders were a flurry of dust in the distance. They had some serious catching up to do, and only a few more miles to do it in.

The water their ponies had drunk seemed to give them just enough extra energy and speed to catch up. Before long, the two friends were again at the tails of the leaders. Now there was only one more steep climb up the last hill, then the gallop into the home valley. All seven leading riders started the climb together, their ponies sweating with effort. Leonie had to grip her pony tightly to avoid falling, but the loss of the saddle meant she was lighter and quicker. She reached the peak first and could hear Jaran and Kubilai screaming encouragement from behind.

She galloped downwards towards the finishing line, the other ponies' hooves ringing in her ears. In a blur, she saw the cheering crowds and the staring faces as the villagers tried to see who was in the lead. "Who is that boy?" they cried.

Just a short distance to go and Leonie saw another rider come up beside her. It was Jaran. "It's your victory, Leonie" he shouted.

"No – we win together!" she shouted – and the two ponies crossed the line, shoulder to shoulder.

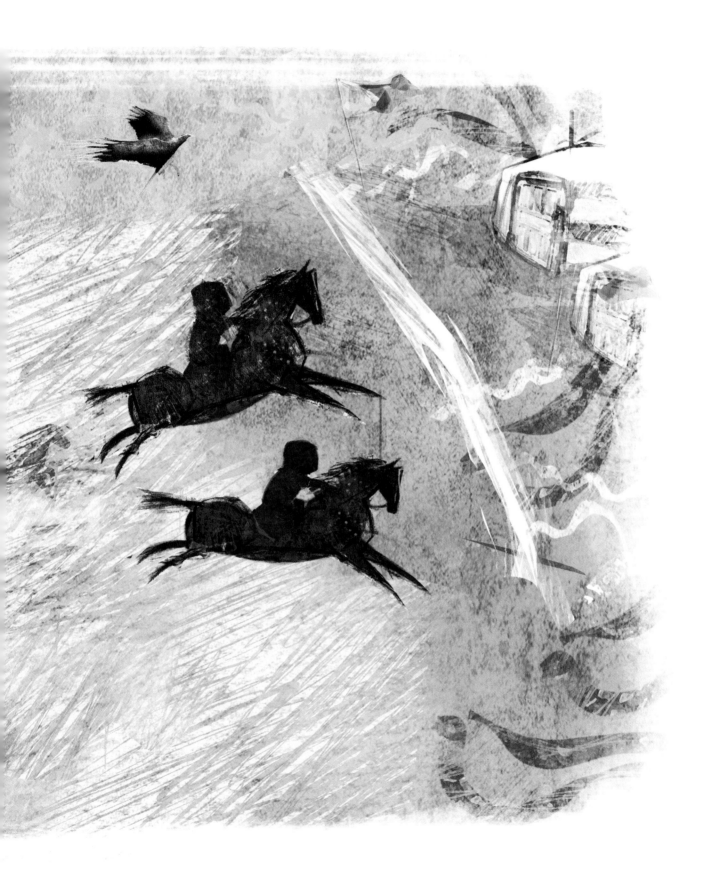

They pulled the ponies to a stop and the villagers ran to crowd around them. "Who is the boy with Jaran?" "Who is the other winner?" they asked. Then Leonie showed her face to the onlookers. Everybody gasped. She looked through the crowd and saw her father staring at her. And then he began to smile, proudly.

"The other winner is my daughter, Leonie" her father announced. "She has indeed the heart of a lioness."

The village chief walked forward to the riders. "Leonie – you have broken the rules" he said. "But perhaps it is time for the rules to change." He turned to the crowd.

"Now I know why there was a rainbow this morning. Leonie has shown that girls can also be great riders. From now on, the Great Race will be open to everyone."

It was a great victory – for Leonie, and for all the girls in the village. Everybody cheered as Kubilai soared above them. Leonie and Jaran hugged their exhausted ponies then fell into each other's arms. In all their lives, they had never been more tired or more happy.

HILARY MOORE

Hilary is a busy mum who works in international business.
She has a PhD and MBA and has published several books.

Most importantly, she is mother of five-year-old Iona - a girl
she hopes will grow up brave and strong, inspired by great girl role models in the books she reads. There aren't many of those great
role models in traditional fairy tales, so Hilary decided
to write some!

100% of the profits from the 'Brave Strong Girls' go to charities that help to educate and empower girls around the world.

CATTY FLORES

Catty was born in Paris but moved to Spain when her family decided to return home. At an early age she began exploring the art of
playing with water, pencils, hands and colours. Catty loved
to redecorate and filled every space she could reach. Needless
to say, her family was horrified.

Fortunately, this mischievousness gave back lots of challenges and satisfaction over the years. The most recent one has been
working on the Brave, Strong Girls series, a beautiful opportunity to help overcome stereotypes and preconceptions."

Catty's artistic playmates have included international publishing houses and advertising agencies like M&C Saatchi London, Gruner
Jahr Mondadori and Helbling Languages.
www.cattyflores.com

The 'Brave Strong Girls' concept
www.bravestronggirls.com

100% of the profits from the 'Brave Strong Girls' series will
go to charities that help to educate and empower girls around the world.

The Brave, Strong Girls series is specially created to give children strong girl role models in the books they read, with female
characters who are resilient, who are brave, and who think for themselves. Fairy tales have a wonderful place in young children's
lives – sparking their imagination and teaching them about life. Unfortunately, the traditional versions are unfair to girls and
women. Almost all the evil characters are older women, jealous of their younger counterparts. The young girl characters are often
judged only on their beauty. They also spend much of their time totally passive – asleep, trapped, or helpless victims. They make silly
mistakes and their only chance of a happy ending is to be rescued by, or married to, a prince.

We know this does not reflect reality, and the Brave, Strong Girls Series is putting this right! It's a series for girls and boys - both
gain a lot from seeing female characters they can respect. The books are fun and beautifully illustrated. They keep the magic and
beauty of the traditional fairytales, while also sending much better messages about the amazing talents and courage of girls and
women.

Also in this series:

Brave, Strong Snow White and the Seven Dwarfs
and
The Brave Strong Mermaid

14816858R00015

Printed in Great Britain
by Amazon.co.uk, Ltd.,
Marston Gate.